The Flamingo
Who Forgot

ReadZone Books Limited

First published in this edition 2015

© in this edition ReadZone Books Limited 2015
© in text Alan Durant 2007
© in illustrations Franco Rivolli 2007

Alan Durant has asserted his right under the Copyright Designs and Patents Act 1988 to be identified as the author of this work.

Franco Rivolli has asserted his right under the Copyright Designs and Patents Act 1988 to be identified as the illustrator of this work.

Every attempt has been made by the Publisher to secure appropriate permissions for material reproduced in this book. If there has been any oversight we will be happy to rectify the situation in future editions or reprints. Written submissions should be made to the Publisher.

British Library Cataloguing in Publication Data (CIP) is available for this title.

Printed in Malta by Melita Press.

ISBN 978 1 78322 034 2

Visit our website: www.readzonebooks.com

The Flamingo Who Forgot

Alan Durant
and Franco Rivolli

READZONE

The flamingo stood in
the lake on one leg.

Along trumped an elephant.

'Why are you standing on one leg?' he asked.

'So that I don't forget,' said the flamingo.

'Elephants never forget,' said the elephant. 'What are you trying to remember?'

The flamingo frowned. 'I've forgotten,' she said.

'Oh, well perhaps I can help,' said the elephant. 'It's bath day today, you know. Perhaps that's what you wanted to remember.' He squirted water into the air.

The flamingo shook her head. 'I bathe everyday,' she said. 'That's not what I've forgotten. But thanks for your help.'

A monkey waltzed by.
'Say, why are you standing
like that?' he asked.

'To remember something,'
said the flamingo. 'But I've
forgotten what.'

'Well, isn't that crazy?' said the
monkey. 'But don't worry, I can help.
It's the Jungle Dance Contest today.
That's what you wanted to
remember.'

The flamingo shook her head.
'Flamingos don't dance,' she said.
'That's not what I've forgotten.
But thanks for your help.'

13

Just then a cockatoo flew by.

'Hey. Don't you look funny,' she said.

'I'm trying to remember something important,' said the flamingo again. 'But I've forgotten what.'

The cockatoo chuckled. 'I can help you there,' she said. 'It's national nest-building day. That's what you're trying to remember.' The cockatoo picked up some twigs and flew up into a tree.

The flamingo shook her head. 'I live in the water and my nest is made of mud,' she said. 'That's not what I've forgotten. But thanks for your help.'

A hyena was the next to stop by. But he was no help at all. All he did was laugh and laugh – and the poor flamingo went pinker than ever.

A fish popped up from under the water.

'Are you the finishing post?' he asked.

'No,' said the flamingo. 'I'm standing on one leg like this to remember something important. But I've forgotten what.'

'Oh,' said the fish with a flick-flack-swish. 'Today's the Lake Swimming Gala. I expect you were trying to remember that.'

The flamingo shook her head. 'I can't swim,' she said. 'I'm sure that's not what I've forgotten. But thanks for your help.'

The flamingo stood in the lake on one leg, feeling very silly for being so forgetful.

Along came another flamingo, carrying a parcel.

'Hello, Fedora,' he said. 'I see you're trying to remember something.'

'That's right, Fred,' she sighed. 'But I've forgotten what.'

Fred smiled. 'Perhaps I can help,' he said and he handed Fedora the parcel.

'For me?' she said.

'For you,' said Fred.

Suddenly Fedora smiled so much she went bright pink with happiness.

'At last I've remembered!' she cried – and she put her leg down. 'What I wanted to remember is that today's…

… my birthday!'

'Happy birthday!' said Fred.

Then Fedora the flamingo
had a birthday that she would
never forget!

Did you enjoy this book?

Look out for more *Swifts* titles –
stories in 500 words to build confidence

The Flamingo who Forgot by Alan Durant and Franco Rivolli
ISBN 978 1 78322 034 2

George and the Dragonfly by Andy Blackford and Sue Mason
ISBN 978 1 78322 168 4

Glub! by Penny Little and Sue Mason
ISBN 978 1 78322 035 9

The Grumpy Queen by Valerie Wilding and Simona Sanfilippo
ISBN 978 1 78322 166 0

The King of Kites by Judith Heneghan and Laure Fournier
ISBN 978 1 78322 164 6

Hoppy Ever After! by Alan Durant and Sue Mason
ISBN 978 1 78322 036 6

Just Custard by Joe Hackett and Alexandra Lolombo
ISBN 978 1 78322 167 7

Space Cadets to the Rescue by Paul Harrison and Sue Mason
ISBN 978 1 78322 039 7

Monster in the Garden by Anne Rooney and Bruno Robert
ISBN 978 1 78322 163 9

Wait a Minute, Ruby! by Mary Chapman and Nick Schon
ISBN 978 1 78322 165 3

The One That Got Away by Paul Harrison and Tim Archbold
ISBN 978 1 78322 037 3

The Perfect Prince by Paul Harrison and Sue Mason
ISBN 978 1 78322 038 0